TABLE OF CONTENT

Chapter 1: The Gates of San Pe

Introduction to San Pedro prison, ...nditions and violence 1

Arrival of Rusty Young and his initial shock at the prison's brutality... 2

Chapter 5: The Company of Wolves 5

Formation of the "Company of Wolves," a group of dangerous and ruthless inmates 5

Rusty's struggle to navigate the complex dynamics within the group... 6

Chapter 6: The Convict Code 10

Unwritten rules and customs that govern life within San Pedro ..10

The importance of respect, loyalty, and violence 12

Chapter 7: The Bleakest Days 15

Rusty's descent into despair and addiction 15

The psychological toll of prolonged imprisonment and isolation . 17

Chapter 8: The Gringo 19

Rusty's experiences as a foreigner in San Pedro 19

The prejudice and discrimination he faces from other inmates....20

Chapter 9: The Road to Redemption 22

Rusty's decision to change his life and escape the prison's grip....22

The challenges and obstacles he faces along the way 24

Chapter 1: The Gates of San Pedro

Introduction to San Pedro prison, known for its extreme conditions and violence

The initial description of the prison, with its grim, weathered walls and the pervasive sense of desperation, immediately sets the stage for the extreme conditions and violence that will define the narrative. Russell, the protagonist, having navigated a labyrinthine network of bribes and connections, finds himself standing on the threshold of a world unlike any he's ever known. His entry into the prison, marked by a disorienting sensory overload and a palpable atmosphere of distrust, serves as a stark reminder of the power dynamics that govern this microcosm of society. He is immediately confronted with the brutal realities of prison life, as witnessed in the relentless hustle and bustle of the prison economy, where every interaction, every transaction, carries the potential for danger. The constant fear of violence permeates the air, palpable in the guarded glances and whispered warnings, creating an undercurrent of paranoia that underscores the precariousness of life within the walls of San Pedro. This tension is further emphasized by the physical presence of armed guards, their watchful eyes a constant reminder of the authority that governs this world. The initial introduction to the prison's hierarchy, with its intricate web of power and influence, highlights the stark reality that inmates are not simply prisoners but participants in a complex, sometimes brutal social system. The chapter concludes with Russell navigating the complexities of this new world, the initial sense of awe and apprehension giving way to a growing awareness of the challenges he will face in the days to come. The reader is left with a chilling glimpse of the brutal, unforgiving reality of life in San Pedro, a microcosm of society where survival is a daily struggle and violence looms as a constant threat. The chapter's closing lines, hinting at the unimaginable horrors that await him, leave a lasting impression, setting the stage for a narrative that will expose the depths of human resilience and the lengths to which individuals will go to survive in the face of extreme adversity. .

.

Arrival of Rusty Young and his initial shock at the prison's brutality

Rusty Young's arrival at San Pedro prison, the notorious maximum-security facility in Bolivia, serves as the stark, brutal introduction to the world of "Marching Powder. " Author Rusty Young, a former British drug smuggler, walks through the prison gates with the weight of his crimes and the uncertainty of his future heavy upon him. The initial shock of the prison's atmosphere is immediate and palpable, a stark contrast to the world Young knew before his incarceration. The air hangs thick with the stench of unwashed bodies, the cacophony of shouts, and the constant threat of violence. Young's initial experience, characterized by fear and confusion, highlights the harsh realities of prison life, where survival becomes an immediate and paramount concern.

The very first image that greets Young upon his arrival is a chilling illustration of the prison's brutal reality. He encounters a man with a severed hand, a gruesome sight that immediately underscores the unforgiving nature of San Pedro. This encounter throws Young into the deep end of the prison's brutal hierarchy, where violence and intimidation are the norm. Young is not merely imprisoned; he is thrown into a world where power dynamics are fluid and survival hinges on an ability to navigate the perilous currents of the prison's underground economy.

The prison's brutality is not limited to physical violence; it extends to the psychological torment experienced by its inmates. Young witnesses firsthand the degrading treatment meted out to prisoners, the constant humiliation, and the relentless reminders of their lost freedom. The prison guards, depicted as callous and indifferent, add to the atmosphere of fear and despair. Young is stripped of his belongings, subjected to invasive searches, and forced to submit to the whims of the prison's hierarchy. This initial experience of dehumanization sets the stage for Young's subsequent struggles and his gradual acclimatization to the harsh realities of prison life.

The prison's physical infrastructure mirrors its brutal nature. The overcrowded, unsanitary conditions contribute to the sense of despair and make it difficult for inmates to maintain their sense of dignity. The cells, described as "filthy and suffocating," are mere cages, offering no semblance of privacy or comfort. The harshness of the environment is further amplified by the constant threat of violence, the omnipresent fear of being targeted by gangs or simply caught in the crossfire of power struggles. This initial encounter with the physical reality of San Pedro serves as a stark reminder of the challenges Young will face during his time in prison.

Young's arrival at San Pedro is not simply a physical transition; it represents a psychological shift. The shock of the prison's brutality serves as a wake-up call, forcing Young to confront the gravity of his situation. His initial naivete gives way to a growing awareness of the dangers and complexities of prison life. The encounter with the severed hand, the degrading treatment by guards, the overwhelming sense of despair—all these experiences contribute to a sense of urgency, a desperate need to adapt and survive within the prison's unforgiving environment. This realization marks the beginning of Young's journey, a journey of survival, adaptation, and ultimately, a struggle for redemption.

The brutal realities of San Pedro are not simply a backdrop for Young's journey; they become the very fabric of his experience. The initial shock of the prison's brutality serves as the catalyst for Young's transformation, his gradual acceptance of the prison's rules, and his eventual embrace of the prison's underground economy. This initial shock sets the stage for the complex tapestry of relationships, challenges, and ultimately, the unexpected opportunities that Young will encounter within the walls of San Pedro. The shock of his arrival serves as a reminder that this is not merely a place of confinement but a world unto itself, a world where survival depends on the ability to navigate its brutal realities.

.

Chapter 5: The Company of Wolves

Formation of the "Company of Wolves," a group of dangerous and ruthless inmates

The formation of the "Company of Wolves" within the unforgiving landscape of San Pedro prison in Bolivia, as detailed in Rusty Young's "Marching Powder," is not a sudden eruption of violence but a gradual, chilling evolution of the prison's brutal power dynamics. It's a testament to the human capacity for adaptation to the most extreme of circumstances, where the very principles of morality are warped to accommodate the need for survival. .

The "Company of Wolves" emerges from a pre-existing hierarchy, one built on fear, respect, and ruthlessness. Initially, the prison is ruled by a brutal system of "pumas," inmates who exploit their power through violence and extortion, terrorizing weaker prisoners. This system thrives on an unspoken understanding: comply or face consequences. It is within this oppressive structure that the seeds of the "Company of Wolves" are sown. .

The "Wolves" are not a mere extension of the "pumas" but a manifestation of the inherent flaws of the prison system. They are a response to the endemic corruption and systemic failure within San Pedro's walls. The "pumas," in their pursuit of power and wealth, create a climate of constant fear and distrust. The "Wolves" exploit this vulnerability, capitalizing on the need for protection and offering an alternative, albeit equally ruthless, system of order. .

Their emergence is fueled by the prison's inherent instability. The "pumas," in their pursuit of personal gain, lose sight of the greater picture. Their brutality breeds resentment and an unspoken desire for change. The "Wolves" present themselves as a solution, promising protection from the "pumas" and a fairer distribution of power. Their success lies in their ability to exploit the fear and desperation of the inmates, offering a twisted sense of security in exchange for loyalty and obedience. .

The "Wolves" operate as a network of interconnected cells, each led by a "capo" who maintains absolute authority over his "pack. " This structure, reminiscent of a wolf pack's hierarchical organization, allows them to exert control over the prison with an efficiency unmatched by the fragmented rule of the "pumas. " .

However, the "Wolves" are not merely a group of hardened criminals seeking to exploit the prison system. They are, in a way, a product of it. Their ruthlessness is not solely their own but a consequence of the environment they inhabit. The constant struggle for survival, the deprivation, and the lack of hope instill in them a brutal pragmatism that is both terrifying and undeniably human. .

Their ascent is fueled by a combination of strategic maneuvering, intimidation, and a shared understanding of the prison's brutal reality. They are able to establish a semblance of order amidst chaos, providing a twisted sense of security for those who swear allegiance to them. The "Wolves" represent a brutal yet efficient response to the failing systems of San Pedro, embodying the dark side of human adaptation in the face of adversity. Their rise signifies a shift in the prison's power dynamics, one that will reshape the prison into a landscape of even greater brutality and despair.

Rusty's struggle to navigate the complex dynamics within the group

Rusty's journey within the prison walls of "Marching Powder" is a testament to the complexities of human interaction, especially within the confines of a brutal and unforgiving environment. His struggle to navigate the delicate balance of power, loyalty, and survival within the group, a microcosm of the prison itself, reveals the profound impact of social dynamics on individual agency. Rusty's initial naivety and outsider status are a stark contrast to the hardened realities of prison life. He enters the world of San Pedro, the notorious Bolivian prison, with a degree of idealism, believing that he can retain some semblance of his former life, his status as a drug runner, while simultaneously seeking a different path, one of acceptance and perhaps even redemption. This naivete, however, quickly clashes with the cold realities of prison life, where survival is paramount and social hierarchies are ruthlessly enforced. .

Rusty's first brush with the harsh realities of the prison's social structure comes in the form of his encounter with the "Pachos," a powerful and dangerous gang controlling a significant portion of the prison. Their cold, calculated cruelty, epitomized by their brutal punishments for perceived transgressions, underscores the unforgiving nature of the environment. Rusty's initial attempts to ingratiate himself with the Pachos, offering gifts and seeking their favor, highlight his desperation for acceptance and protection. However, the Pachos are wary of outsiders, especially those perceived as weak or untrustworthy, and their suspicion creates a constant tension in Rusty's interactions with them. This initial rejection from the Pachos creates a sense of isolation for Rusty, who finds himself caught between the need to survive and his desire for belonging.

He then aligns himself with a more nuanced group, the "Venezuelans," who operate under a different set of rules, one based on loyalty, mutual respect, and shared understanding. Rusty finds himself drawn to their camaraderie, their willingness to share their lives and experiences, their vulnerability, their shared humanity. He finds a sense of community within their group, something that he desperately craves. This sense of belonging, however, comes at a price. He is forced to adopt their way of life, a life steeped in violence, deception, and criminality. His participation in the illicit activities of the Venezuelans, from smuggling contraband to engaging in violent confrontations, reveals the gradual erosion of his former self and the dark transformation he undergoes. This transformation is a reflection of his struggle to survive within the prison, a struggle that necessitates a constant negotiation of his values, his morals, and his sense of self.

The dynamics within the group, however, are not static. Power struggles and betrayals are constant, and Rusty's loyalty to the Venezuelans is tested time and again. His struggle to maintain his place within the group, to remain a valuable member, is a constant source of anxiety. He is forced to constantly prove his worth, his loyalty, his ability to contribute. This constant struggle for recognition, for acceptance, highlights the fragility of social bonds within the confines of the prison. The loyalty he offers is often met with skepticism, suspicion, and fear, leaving him constantly vulnerable to betrayal.

Rusty's complex relationship with his "friends" within the Venezuelans further complicates his journey. He is drawn to their camaraderie, their warmth, their genuine connection. However, these bonds are constantly threatened by the inherent dangers of the prison environment. The Venezuelans are involved in a constant battle for power, and loyalty is often tested by the need for survival. His relationships with individuals like "El Gato" and "El Chacal" are characterized by a mix of affection, fear, and distrust. He is drawn to their strength, their charisma, their ability to navigate the harsh realities of the prison. However, he is also aware of their potential to betray him, to use him for their own ends. The tension between trust and suspicion, between loyalty and self-preservation, permeates his relationships with these individuals.

In his quest to survive, Rusty adopts the behaviors and values of the group. He participates in their activities, engages in their rituals, and learns their codes of conduct. This transformation, however, is not without consequences. His descent into the world of drugs, violence, and criminal activity gradually erodes his sense of self, his morals, and his connection to the outside world. He becomes increasingly detached from the life he once knew, his transformation mirroring the harsh realities of the prison.

This transformation is a stark reminder of the power of environment to shape individuals. The prison, with its rigid social hierarchies, its constant threat of violence, its pervasive culture of survival, forces Rusty to adapt. He learns to play the game, to navigate the complex dynamics of the group, to become someone he never thought he could be. His struggle to maintain his humanity within this brutal environment becomes a testament to the resilience of the human spirit, a spirit that is constantly tested, constantly challenged, yet ultimately capable of remarkable adaptation.

Rusty's journey within the prison's intricate web of social dynamics is a powerful narrative of survival, transformation, and the enduring human capacity for resilience. His struggle to navigate the complex power dynamics, to forge connections within the unforgiving confines of the prison, reveals the multifaceted nature of human behavior. He learns to navigate the treacherous waters of prison politics, where loyalty is constantly tested and trust is a precious commodity. The story of Rusty's journey is a stark reminder of the human capacity for both resilience and darkness, a testament to the power of environment to shape individuals, and a haunting exploration of the blurred lines between survival and surrender.

.

Chapter 6: The Convict Code

Unwritten rules and customs that govern life within San Pedro

Within the unforgiving confines of San Pedro, a prison notorious for its brutality and chaotic nature, life is governed not by formal laws but by an intricate web of unwritten rules and customs. These unspoken codes, meticulously crafted and enforced by the inmates themselves, dictate every facet of existence, from the simple act of entering the prison gates to the most intricate power dynamics within its walls. Understanding these rules is not merely a matter of curiosity but a matter of survival. To breach these unspoken boundaries is to invite the wrath of fellow inmates, and potentially, the intervention of the ever-present threat of violence. .

One of the most fundamental principles within San Pedro is the concept of "respect," a highly subjective term that translates into a complex set of behavioral expectations. Respect is earned, not given, and is contingent on numerous factors, including one's social standing, financial resources, and ability to navigate the intricate power dynamics within the prison. Respect can be earned through displays of strength, cunning, or even simply by adhering to the unwritten rules that govern daily life. Conversely, disrespect can be manifested in numerous ways, ranging from casual insults to transgressions of established territories or social hierarchies. An inmate who lacks respect is seen as vulnerable, a prime target for exploitation and violence. .

The intricate web of unwritten rules that governs the flow of life within San Pedro encompasses far more than simply respect. The very structure of the prison itself reflects the presence of an invisible hierarchy. The prison's layout, with its distinct "pavilions" and "blocks" serving as segregated social and economic strata, is a testament to this hidden order. Within these divisions, further hierarchies exist, with "pateros," or powerful leaders, wielding significant influence over the lives of their subordinates. These leaders, often possessing a combination of charisma, financial resources, and a willingness to employ violence, act as brokers, mediating disputes, negotiating deals, and controlling the flow of goods and services within their domains. .

The concept of "minding your own business" is paramount within San Pedro's unwritten code. Interfering in affairs that do not directly concern you can lead to unwanted attention, and potentially, retaliation. The prison fosters a culture of self-reliance, where individuals are responsible for their own safety and well-being. This does not, however, equate to isolation. The prison, despite its brutal realities, also fosters a sense of community, particularly within the "pavilions" and "blocks. " A shared sense of vulnerability and a need for mutual support contribute to a complex tapestry of alliances and rivalries that dictate the daily rhythm of life within the prison walls.

Within this unforgiving environment, the concept of "justice" operates on a distinct set of principles. The official legal system, with its bureaucratic procedures and often-inconsistent application, is viewed with deep suspicion. Justice within San Pedro is often swift and brutal, meted out by the inmates themselves, in response to perceived transgressions. "Trials" are often informal, conducted within the confines of a single "pavilion" or "block," with the verdict dictated by the prevailing power dynamic. While this informal system may seem inherently unfair, it serves a pragmatic purpose. It offers a sense of immediate consequence, deterring future transgressions and maintaining a semblance of order within the chaotic reality of prison life.

The unwritten rules that govern life within San Pedro are not static. They are constantly evolving, adapting to the shifting power dynamics and the arrival of new inmates. The ability to learn and adapt to these ever-changing rules is crucial for survival. An inmate who remains inflexible, clinging to outdated norms or failing to recognize the subtle shifts in social dynamics, risks isolation, exploitation, or even worse. The prison, in this sense, is a microcosm of society itself, where the unwritten rules that govern daily life are just as important as the formal laws that are meant to govern behavior.

The unwritten rules of San Pedro, though brutal and often unfair, offer a glimpse into the human capacity for adaptation, resilience, and even a fragile sense of community. They reveal how individuals, stripped of their liberty and forced to navigate a hostile and uncertain environment, create their own social constructs, their own laws, and their own fragile sense of order within the chaos. These unspoken codes are a testament to the human spirit's ability to forge meaning and purpose even within the darkest of circumstances. They represent a desperate attempt to find order and security in a world where both are scarce commodities.

The importance of respect, loyalty, and violence

The heart of "Marching Powder" beats with the pulse of a harsh reality: survival within the confines of a brutal, South American prison. The book's sixth chapter, aptly titled "The Convict Code," delves into the intricate web of unspoken rules, forged in the fires of violence and desperation, that govern life behind bars. Respect, loyalty, and violence, interwoven in a complex tapestry, form the bedrock of this code. They are not mere concepts but tangible forces, shaping every interaction, every decision, every breath within the prison walls.

Respect, in this context, transcends mere courtesy. It is a currency earned through strength, cunning, and a willingness to stand one's ground. It is bestowed upon those who command fear and loyalty, who can navigate the treacherous waters of prison life with a steady hand. It is a shield against exploitation, a badge of honor, and a currency that can buy safety, influence, and even a semblance of freedom within the prison's iron grip. Respect, however, is a fragile commodity. It can be gained through acts of bravery or lost in an instant, a fleeting whisper in the face of a perceived slight or betrayal. It is a constant struggle, a dance on a razor's edge, demanding unwavering vigilance and an understanding of the nuanced language of prison society.

Loyalty is the glue that binds inmates together, forming fragile alliances in the face of a hostile and unpredictable environment. It is the promise of protection, the unwavering support in times of need, the shared burden of survival in a world where trust is a rare and precious commodity. It is tested relentlessly, challenged by fear, greed, and the constant threat of betrayal. Loyalty, like respect, is not a given; it is earned through actions, through shared experiences, through the unwavering commitment to a cause, whether it be protecting a fellow inmate from violence or standing by them in the face of an unjust accusation. It is a bond forged in the crucible of adversity, a lifeline in a sea of despair. .

But the shadow of violence looms large over the prison's intricate social fabric. Violence is not simply a means of resolving disputes, but a language, a threat, and a tool of control. It is a constant undercurrent, a palpable tension that permeates every interaction. It is used to enforce respect, to punish betrayal, to maintain order, and to settle scores. Violence can be a chilling display of power, a swift and merciless judgment, or a slow and agonizing torture. It is a constant reminder of the fragility of life, the precarious nature of safety, and the brutal reality of existence within prison walls. .

The Convict Code is a testament to the human capacity for adaptation, for creating order in chaos, for forging bonds in the face of unimaginable adversity. It is a brutal reflection of the realities of prison life, a testament to the power of respect, the fragility of loyalty, and the chilling pervasiveness of violence. "Marching Powder" does not shy away from the stark reality of the prison world, but rather shines a light on the intricate social structures that emerge within it, revealing the human spirit's resilience in the face of deprivation and brutality. It is a reminder that even in the most unforgiving of environments, respect, loyalty, and violence, intertwined in a complex dance, shape the fabric of human interaction..

.

Chapter 7: The Bleakest Days

Rusty's descent into despair and addiction

Chapter 7, aptly titled "The Bleakest Days," paints a harrowing portrait of Rusty's descent into despair and addiction. The chapter marks a turning point in the narrative, a stark shift from Rusty's initial naivety and optimism to a crushing reality of prison life that gnaws at his soul. This descent is not sudden, but rather a slow, insidious erosion of hope, fuelled by the suffocating atmosphere of La Paz prison and the relentless onslaught of misery surrounding him. .

The chapter opens with a chilling description of the prison's harsh environment: the stifling heat, the constant threat of violence, the relentless boredom, and the pervasive stench of desperation. This setting serves as the perfect breeding ground for despair, a constant reminder of the grim reality that Rusty is trapped in. This despair manifests itself in Rusty's growing disillusionment with the prison system and his perceived lack of control over his own life. He feels helpless, a pawn in a game played by corrupt guards and manipulative inmates. He questions his own sanity, wondering if he will ever be able to escape the clutches of this living nightmare.

Rusty's despair is further fuelled by the rampant drug use within the prison walls. He witnesses firsthand the devastating effects of addiction on his fellow inmates, their bodies ravaged by the relentless cycle of abuse and withdrawal. This constant exposure to the horrors of addiction, coupled with his own feelings of helplessness and despair, slowly pushes Rusty towards a dangerous path.

The book delves into the insidious nature of drug use within the prison walls. Rusty initially resists, viewing it as a path to further misery. Yet, the relentless pressure from his fellow inmates, coupled with his own growing despair, eventually chip away at his resistance. He is drawn to the temporary escape that drugs offer, a fleeting respite from the crushing reality of his prison existence. The allure of oblivion becomes too powerful to resist.

The turning point comes with the arrival of the "Red Devils," a group of inmates notorious for their brutality and drug trade. Their presence intensifies the already oppressive atmosphere, adding a layer of fear and paranoia to Rusty's daily life. He witnesses the power they wield, their ability to manipulate and control the prison's hierarchy, a stark reminder of the vulnerability he faces within the prison walls.

The Red Devils' influence is not only limited to the prison's social structure, but it also extends to the drug trade. Rusty observes their ruthless operations, the constant flow of drugs into the prison, and the desperation of inmates vying for a fix. He finds himself drawn to the allure of escape, the promise of a temporary reprieve from the harsh realities of his existence.

This environment of despair and desperation creates the perfect storm for Rusty's descent into addiction. The constant pressure, the lack of hope, the fear of violence, and the pervasive presence of drugs all contribute to his eventual surrender. He succumbs to the lure of temporary escape, finding solace in the fleeting euphoria that drugs provide.

The chapter concludes with Rusty's first encounter with the drug that will come to define his prison experience: cocaine. He is drawn to its powerful effect, the instant euphoria that washes over him, a temporary escape from the harsh realities of his prison existence. The book portrays this initial encounter not as a celebratory moment but as a tragic turning point, a fateful step down a path that will lead him deeper into the abyss of addiction. .

The bleakest days have arrived, and Rusty finds himself trapped in a cycle of despair and addiction. The once bright spark of hope within him is slowly being extinguished, replaced by the cold reality of his prison existence and the ever-present shadow of his own self-destruction. The chapter serves as a poignant reminder of the devastating power of despair and the insidious allure of addiction, and how these forces can even shatter the spirit of a man like Rusty, who initially entered prison with hope and a strong sense of self.

The psychological toll of prolonged imprisonment and isolation

Within the chilling confines of San Pedro Prison, a microcosm of humanity's resilience and despair unfolds, echoing the profound psychological toll of prolonged imprisonment and isolation. Chapter 7, "The Bleakest Days," delves into the heart of this torment, exposing the insidious nature of confinement and its capacity to warp the very fabric of the human psyche. The narrative unflinchingly paints a portrait of men stripped of their freedom, their existence reduced to a monotonous cycle of routine and uncertainty. .

The prison's oppressive atmosphere, a suffocating blend of cramped cells, stifling heat, and the constant threat of violence, acts as a catalyst for psychological decay. The constant threat of danger and the inherent powerlessness of the inmates create a pervasive sense of anxiety, chipping away at their mental fortitude. The monotony of daily life, devoid of meaningful engagement or hope, becomes a relentless assault on their spirits. The book vividly illustrates the psychological torment of prolonged imprisonment, capturing the despair of men trapped in a cycle of relentless fear and uncertainty.

The chapter's exploration of the "Bleakest Days" highlights the profound impact of isolation on the human psyche. Deprived of meaningful social connections, inmates are left to grapple with their own thoughts and emotions. The absence of familiar faces, the silence that permeates the prison, and the constant sense of being watched contribute to a deep sense of loneliness and despair. The book underscores the importance of human connection, revealing how isolation can unravel the very foundation of mental wellbeing, leaving individuals vulnerable to mental health issues and a profound sense of alienation.

"Marching Powder" delves into the psychological depths of the inmates' experiences, showcasing how prolonged isolation can exacerbate existing mental health conditions or trigger new ones. The chapter reveals how the absence of familiar routines, the loss of control over one's environment, and the perpetual threat of violence can fuel feelings of paranoia, anxiety, and depression. The book underscores the human vulnerability to psychological strain, highlighting the devastating impact of confinement on the inmates' mental states. .

The book offers a poignant examination of the complex relationship between isolation and identity, revealing how the enforced separation from the outside world can lead to a profound sense of self-doubt and a loss of personal meaning. Confined within the prison walls, inmates grapple with the realization that their lives have been irrevocably altered, their former identities eclipsed by the harsh realities of their incarceration. This struggle to reconcile their past selves with their present circumstances becomes a source of immense psychological distress, driving them into a labyrinth of despair.

"Marching Powder" provides a stark reminder that imprisonment, particularly prolonged imprisonment, is not merely a physical restraint but a profound psychological torment. The chapter, "The Bleakest Days," offers a chilling glimpse into the depths of despair that can arise from prolonged confinement and isolation, revealing the profound impact on the human psyche. The book leaves readers with an indelible understanding of the psychological toll of imprisonment, highlighting the imperative to acknowledge and address the complex mental health challenges faced by those behind bars. .

.

Chapter 8: The Gringo

Rusty's experiences as a foreigner in San Pedro

Rusty's journey as a foreigner in San Pedro prison, as detailed in "Marching Powder: A Journey Through Prison Life," paints a vivid picture of the complexities and challenges of navigating a foreign culture within a confined and often brutal environment. He arrives with an outsider's perspective, initially overwhelmed by the sheer scale and chaotic nature of the prison. Rusty's status as a foreigner, while initially a source of curiosity and amusement, quickly becomes a source of vulnerability. The lack of common language, cultural understanding, and established connections within the prison hierarchy creates a sense of isolation and vulnerability. He is forced to rely on his wit, resourcefulness, and, to a degree, his foreignness as a bargaining chip. He adapts, learns, and grows, navigating the intricate social dynamics and power structures of San Pedro. His ability to speak Spanish, albeit imperfectly, becomes a valuable asset, allowing him to communicate and build relationships. He embraces local customs and traditions, even participating in the prison's unique economic system, trading and selling goods to make a living. However, his foreigner status, coupled with the inherent dangers of a prison environment, makes him a target for exploitation and danger. He faces constant scrutiny, suspicion, and even threats from inmates and guards alike. He learns the importance of discretion and vigilance, understanding that any misstep or perceived weakness could have dire consequences. The book's perspective reveals the unique perspective of a foreigner in a foreign prison, navigating a harsh reality where survival depends on a delicate balance of cunning, adaptability, and a constant awareness of one's vulnerability. Rusty's journey highlights the challenges and opportunities that arise when an individual is thrust into an unfamiliar world, forced to adapt and find his place within a society that is both alien and unforgiving. His experience transcends a mere physical confinement, revealing the psychological and emotional toll of living within a microcosm of society where the rules, hierarchies, and power dynamics are vastly different from those he knew before. .

.

The prejudice and discrimination he faces from other inmates

In the harrowing account of his imprisonment within the notorious San Pedro prison, Rusty Young, the protagonist of "Marching Powder," encounters a labyrinth of prejudice and discrimination, fueled by the potent cocktail of fear, suspicion, and cultural misunderstandings that permeate the prison's volatile ecosystem. The label "gringo," a term laden with historical baggage and societal biases, becomes a badge of suspicion and alienation, branding Rusty as an outsider in a society built on rigid hierarchies and deeply entrenched cultural norms. The inmates, hardened by the unforgiving realities of their confinement, view Rusty with a mixture of curiosity, suspicion, and outright hostility, their perception of him shaped by a myriad of factors that transcend mere nationality.

Rusty's outsider status becomes a constant source of tension and discomfort, amplifying the challenges he faces in navigating the prison's complex social landscape. The inmates' perception of him as a "gringo" fuels a sense of distrust and animosity, leading to a myriad of discriminatory behaviors that range from subtle social exclusion to overt acts of aggression. The prisoners, many of whom have endured years of poverty, injustice, and societal marginalization, see Rusty as an embodiment of the privileges and advantages they perceive the outside world to offer, further fueling their resentment and mistrust.

The inherent prejudice and discrimination Rusty faces from his fellow inmates is not simply a matter of individual bias but rather a reflection of the deeply ingrained cultural and societal realities of Bolivian society, where the "gringo" is often stereotyped as wealthy, privileged, and exploitative. This ingrained prejudice is exacerbated by the prison's environment, a microcosm of societal inequalities and power dynamics, where alliances are formed based on shared backgrounds, experiences, and perceived loyalties. Rusty's lack of familiarity with the prison's unspoken rules and social codes, coupled with his perceived outsider status, makes him an easy target for exploitation and manipulation by those seeking to assert their dominance or extract personal gain.

Rusty's struggles to overcome the prejudice and discrimination he faces serve as a poignant reminder of the universal human need for belonging, the importance of understanding and empathy, and the enduring power of cultural biases to shape our perceptions and actions. The book highlights the human cost of prejudice, illustrating how ingrained stereotypes can lead to isolation, fear, and violence, perpetuating a cycle of animosity and distrust. Rusty's journey through the prison's labyrinth of prejudice and discrimination underscores the critical need for dialogue, understanding, and human connection, even in the harshest and most challenging of environments. .

Chapter 9: The Road to Redemption

Rusty's decision to change his life and escape the prison's grip

The ninth chapter of "Marching Powder," titled "The Road to Redemption," is a pivotal moment in Rusty's journey through the brutal reality of San Pedro prison. It is here that Rusty's internal struggle reaches a critical juncture. The narrative delves into the complexities of his decision to break free from the prison's grip, not just physically, but also mentally and emotionally. The chapter does not simply present Rusty's escape as a physical act but delves into the profound psychological and spiritual transformation that drives it. .

Rusty's decision is born from a potent cocktail of desperation and an unwavering desire for a life beyond the prison walls. The relentless struggle for survival, the constant threat of violence, and the suffocating sense of entrapment all contribute to his yearning for liberation. But it is not just an escape from the physical confines of the prison that Rusty craves; it is an escape from the suffocating grip of the prison's culture, its rules, and its inherent sense of hopelessness.

The chapter explores the nuances of Rusty's decision through his internal monologue, revealing his internal struggles. He grapples with the fear of failure, the uncertainty of the outside world, and the guilt he carries for his past actions. Rusty's decision is not a impulsive act but a carefully considered choice, driven by a deeply rooted desire for redemption.

Rusty's journey is not merely a quest for freedom; it is a journey towards self-discovery and self-forgiveness. The chapter delves into the complex interplay between his desire for freedom and his need to make amends for his past mistakes. It highlights the transformative power of introspection and the possibility of finding redemption even within the harsh realities of prison life.

I masterfully portrays Rusty's internal struggle, illustrating the human capacity for resilience and transformation even in the face of seemingly insurmountable challenges. Rusty's decision to change his life is not just an act of defiance against the prison system; it is a testament to the enduring power of the human spirit. The narrative explores the complexities of human nature, revealing the vulnerability and resilience that coexist within each individual.

The decision to escape is a turning point in Rusty's story. It marks the beginning of his journey towards a new life, one that is free from the constraints of the prison. The chapter meticulously crafts a narrative that transcends the mere act of escaping; it delves into the psychological and emotional turmoil that propels Rusty's decision. .

The chapter also subtly underscores the stark realities of prison life and the limitations imposed on inmates. Rusty's journey is not just a personal one; it reflects the systemic failures and injustices that plague prison systems worldwide. Through Rusty's experience, the chapter raises questions about the human cost of incarceration and the possibility of true redemption within a system that often fails to provide it.

Rusty's decision to change his life is not a simple act of defiance but a profound testament to the human spirit's capacity for transformation. The chapter paints a nuanced portrait of his internal struggles, highlighting the complexities of human nature and the enduring power of hope. It offers a glimpse into the realities of prison life, raising questions about the systemic injustices that plague correctional systems and the possibility of true redemption within those systems. .

The challenges and obstacles he faces along the way

The path to redemption in "Marching Powder" is fraught with formidable challenges, each demanding a unique kind of resilience from Rusty. His journey within the confines of San Pedro prison is a constant struggle against the oppressive system, the brutal realities of prison life, and his own internal demons. Rusty's first major obstacle is the overwhelming sensory overload that greets him upon entering the prison. The prison itself is a chaotic microcosm of human desperation, a tapestry of noise, smells, and visual stimuli that assault the senses. This relentless barrage, combined with the unfamiliar environment, throws Rusty off balance, leaving him vulnerable and disoriented. He must adapt to the relentless cacophony, the suffocating heat, and the constant jostling of bodies in close quarters, all while grappling with the realization that he is trapped in a world he never could have imagined.

The prison's physical limitations are but one layer of the challenge. Rusty faces a much deeper struggle against the systemic corruption and brutality that permeate every aspect of San Pedro. The prison guards are not guardians of justice but agents of chaos, abusing their power to extort and intimidate prisoners. This environment breeds a culture of fear and suspicion, forcing Rusty to navigate a treacherous social landscape where trust is a luxury he cannot afford. The constant threat of violence, whether from fellow inmates or the guards, forces him to constantly be on edge, constantly strategizing his survival. He must learn to read the subtle cues of the prison's social hierarchy, to discern the true nature of his fellow inmates, and to anticipate the unpredictable whims of those who hold the power.

Rusty's path to redemption is further complicated by the inherent contradictions within San Pedro's social structure. While seemingly offering a semblance of autonomy, the prison is a breeding ground for criminal enterprises, where violence and exploitation are the currencies of power. This duality creates a moral dilemma for Rusty. On one hand, he must navigate this complex system to survive, often aligning himself with individuals he would ordinarily condemn. On the other, his moral compass constantly battles with the compromises he must make to stay alive. He grapples with the realization that his pursuit of redemption requires him to engage with the very darkness he seeks to overcome, forcing him to confront the ethical complexities of his situation.

Rusty's internal struggles add another layer of complexity to his quest for redemption. He must battle his own demons, the guilt and shame of his past actions, while simultaneously adapting to the harsh realities of his current situation. He is forced to confront his own weaknesses, his dependence on drugs, and the fear that he may never be able to truly break free from the cycle of addiction. The isolation of prison, the lack of support from the outside world, and the constant reminders of his past mistakes threaten to break his spirit. He is left wrestling with his own mortality, with the possibility that redemption may be a distant dream, a mirage that fades in the heat of his despair.

Rusty's journey towards redemption is not a linear progression but a constant struggle against the forces that seek to keep him trapped. He must navigate the treacherous landscape of San Pedro, a place where violence, corruption, and exploitation are the norm. He must battle his own internal demons, the guilt and shame of his past, and the fear of losing his humanity within the prison's walls. Rusty's path to redemption is a testament to the power of hope and the resilience of the human spirit. It is a reminder that even in the darkest of places, even in the face of overwhelming odds, the possibility of change, of redemption, always exists. .

.

Printed in Great Britain
by Amazon